White Fang

LEVEL TWO   **700 HEADWORDS**

OXFORD
UNIVERSITY PRESS

Great Clarendon Street, Oxford OX2 6DP

Oxford University Press is a department of the University of Oxford.
It furthers the University's objective of excellence in research, scholarship,
and education by publishing worldwide in

Oxford New York

Auckland Cape Town Dar es Salaam Hong Kong Karachi
Kuala Lumpur Madrid Melbourne Mexico City Nairobi
New Delhi Shanghai Taipei Toronto

With offices in

Argentina Austria Brazil Chile Czech Republic France Greece
Guatemala Hungary Italy Japan Poland Portugal Singapore
South Korea Switzerland Thailand Turkey Ukraine Vietnam

OXFORD and OXFORD ENGLISH are registered trade marks of
Oxford University Press in the UK and in certain other countries

ACKNOWLEDGEMENTS

Illustrations by: David Frankland

The publisher would like to thank the following for permission to reproduce photographs: Ardea pp iv
(Wolf/Francois Gohier), iv (West Highland Terrier/John Daniels), (Weasel/Chris Knights),
iv (Guinea pig/Pat Morris), iv (Lynx/Johan de Meester), iv (Moose/John Cancalosi), iv (Jersey
cow/John Daniels), (Wolf/Francois Gohier), 56 (Black dog/John Daniels), 56 (Goldfish/Brian
Bevan), 56 (Common frog/Brian Bevan), 56 (Golden Retriever/John Daniels), 57 (White
rat/John Daniels), 57 (Grey parrot/John Daniels), 57 (Chimpanzee/Chris Martin Bahr), 57
(Iguana/John Daniels), 57 (Corn snake/John Daniels), 57 (Puppy in basket/John Daniels),
57 (Kitten/John Daniels); Corbis pp 25 (Native Americans/Hulton-Deutsch Collection),
31 (Native American home); Kobal Collection p iv (Free Willy/Warner Bros); Moviestore
Collection p iv (Born Free); NHPA pp 56 (Boy holding python/Joe Blossom), 58 (Orangutan
cradling young/Martin Harvey), 58 (Logger/Martin Harvey), 59 (Orangutan baby/Andy
Rouse), 60 (Lion cubs/Ann & Steve Toon), 60 (Lion tamer with lion/Patrick Fagot), 60 (Caged
African lion/Joe Blossom), 60 (African lions/Jonathan & Angela Scott); OUP p 60 (Journalist/
Photodisc); Oxford Scientific (OSF) pp iv (Shorthair kitten/Mario Mage), 59 (Feeding an
orangutan/Charles Tyler), 59 (Two young orangutans/Konrad Wothe), 59 (orangutans
swinging in trees/Mike Hill).

DOMINOES

Series Editors: Bill Bowler and Sue Parminter

White Fang

Jack London

Text adaptation by John Escott

Illustrated by David Frankland

Jack London (1876–1916) was born in San Francisco, California. He came from a poor family and had many jobs before travelling north to the Yukon in 1897, like many other men, in search of gold. He became famous after writing *The Call of the Wild* in 1903, which tells the story of a sled-dog in the Yukon who leaves his owner to become a wolf in the wild. *White Fang* (1906) tells the story of a wolf that leaves his wild life in the cold and snow of the North to become a dog.

OXFORD
UNIVERSITY PRESS

BEFORE YOU READ

1 **Which of these animals are domestic? Which are wild?**

		Domestic	Wild
1	a wolf	☐	☐
2	a dog	☐	☐
3	a weasel	☐	☐
4	a guinea-pig	☐	☐
5	a cat	☐	☐
6	a lynx	☐	☐
7	a moose	☐	☐
8	a cow	☐	☐

2 **Do you know these animal stories? What must the animals in them learn about? What must they forget about?**

White Fang a wolf learns to be a dog

Free Willy a boy frees a whale from a water park

Born Free Elsa, a lion living with people, learns to be wild

a Taking food from people

b Looking for food without help

c Hunting and killing and escaping from hunters and killers

d Playing

e Having freedom and lots of space to move around in

f Living in a small space and not moving around much

Chapter 1
The She-Wolf

The **land** was white and silent, and without life. This was the Arctic. But there was life on the land. A group of dogs pulled a **sled**, and on the sled was a long, narrow box. In front of the dogs, a man walked with his head down against the cold. Another man walked behind the sled.

A third man was in the box. Dead. He was a young English **lord** and they were taking him across country for his **funeral**.

The thin light of the day was going fast when they heard the first soft, far-away cry. The front man turned and looked at the man behind. Then came a second cry, and a third.

land country

sled a kind of car on skis that dogs pull, for travelling on snow

lord an important, rich man

funeral the time when a dead person is buried

'They're coming after us, Bill,' the front man said.

'They want food, Henry,' his friend answered.

When it was dark, they made their **camp** under some trees, and both men and dogs stayed near the fire.

'How many dogs have we got, Henry?' Bill asked.

'Six,' Henry replied.

'Well, I took six fish out of the bag to feed them,' Bill said. 'And Big Ear didn't get any fish.'

'But there's only six dogs now,' Henry said.

'Well, I saw seven,' Bill said. 'The other one ran away.'

Henry finished eating, then said, 'Was it . . .' A long, sad cry came from somewhere out in the darkness. '. . . a **wolf**?'

The cries of wolves came from every side. Suddenly, Bill saw **a pair of** eyes in the darkness. Henry saw them, too. Soon there was a circle of eyes around their camp.

camp a place where people live in tents for a short time

wolf (*plural* **wolves**) a wild animal like a dog

a pair of two things of the same kind

2

The two men slept side by side. The fire burned down and the circle of eyes got nearer.

In the morning, Henry was first to wake up. It was still dark. Bill got ready to move on while Henry made breakfast.

'How many dogs did you say we had?' Bill asked suddenly.

'Six,' Henry told him.

'Well, there are five now. Fatty ran away in the night.'

After breakfast, they started their journey again. Daylight came at nine o'clock, and in the middle of the day the sky to the south turned red. But the colour did not stay long. By three o'clock, the Arctic night was back across the silent land again.

The cries of the wolves got nearer with the darkness. The two men made camp and ate their meal. Bill went to give the dogs their food. Suddenly, there was the cry of an animal in **pain**. Something moved across the snow into the darkness. Bill was standing with the dogs, half a fish in one hand and a big **stick** in the other.

'It got half the fish,' he said. 'But I hit it.'

In the morning, when Henry woke up, Bill was with the dogs.

'Frog's gone,' Bill said. 'And he was our strongest dog.'

That day was the same as the other days. The men moved across the cold, white world without speaking. The dogs pulled the sled with the dead man on it. That night, Bill **tied** the dogs to a tree. Then the two men sat by their fire.

A sound made them turn round. A wolf moved slowly across the snow to the dogs. One Ear tried to pull away from the tree to get to the wolf.

'It's a she-wolf, Bill!' Henry said. 'I see how it works now. She gets a dog to follow her, then the other wolves jump on it and eat it. That's what happened to Frog and Fatty.'

A noise came from the fire and the she-wolf ran back into the darkness.

pain the feeling that you have in your body when you are hurt

stick a long piece of wood

tie to keep something in one place with rope

In the morning, Henry cooked breakfast, then woke Bill.

'Spanker's gone,' he said. 'He broke his **rope** and the wolves have him now.'

Light came at nine o'clock. At twelve o'clock there was sun in the south. Then came the grey afternoon. Henry was behind the sled. He gave a **whistle**, and Bill turned and looked. The she-wolf was following about a hundred metres behind them. When they stopped, the she-wolf stopped.

'What a strange colour!' Bill said. 'I've never seen a red wolf before.' He got his gun from the sled, but the wolf ran away.

They made their camp early that night. The dogs were tired, but there were still three of them in the morning. In the middle of the day the sled turned over. While the men were trying to turn it up the right way, One Ear ran away across the snow.

The she-wolf was waiting. A minute later, about ten more wolves came out of the trees. They ran after One Ear, and Bill quickly got his gun from the sled and ran after them.

Soon after, Henry heard the sound of the gun. Three times. He heard the angry **growling** of the wolves. A minute later he heard One Ear's cry of pain, and a man's scream.

And that was all. The land was silent again.

Henry sat for a long time on the sled.

rope a very thick strong string

whistle a musical noise that you can make with your mouth

growl to make a deep angry noise

4

At last he got up and tied the two dogs to the sled. But he did not go far. As soon as it started to get dark, he stopped and made his camp for the night.

He made a fire, and the two dogs slept near him. He could see the circle of wolves in the darkness, and he did not sleep.

Next morning he used some rope to pull the long box up into the trees.

'They got Bill, and perhaps they'll get me,' he said to the dead lord. 'But they won't get you, young man.'

The she-wolf followed them all that day, and she was there again that night. It was too dangerous to sleep, so Henry made a big fire and sat beside it with the dogs. The she-wolf watched him, only a metre or two away. Henry took a stick from the fire and threw it at her, and she showed her **fangs** and moved away.

In the morning Henry tried to get to the sled, but the she-wolf jumped at him. It was now too dangerous to leave the fire.

He sat there for two days and two nights, throwing sticks from the fire when the wolves tried to get to him. Once, he felt the she-wolf's teeth on his arm.

At last, he was too tired to fight them off and he went to sleep. He woke once, and saw the she-wolf watching him. Then he woke again, a little later. Something was different.

Suddenly he understood. The wolves weren't there!

He heard the sound of men and sleds in the snow. Minutes later, they stopped at his camp in the trees.

'Red she-wolf . . .' Henry told them. 'First she ate the dog food, then she ate the dogs . . . after that, she ate Bill . . .'

'Where's Lord Alfred?' one of the men asked.

'In a tree,' Henry answered. 'Dead, and in a box.'

And then his eyes closed, and he was asleep again.

Far away came the cry of the hungry wolves looking for food.

fang a long tooth

READING CHECK

Are these sentences true or false? Tick the boxes.

		True	False
a	There are four men and six dogs at the start of the story.	☐	☑
b	They are going across country to a party.	☐	☐
c	Wolves are coming after them.	☐	☐
d	The wolves don't come near at night because of the fire.	☐	☐
e	The dogs leave the men one by one and follow the she-wolf.	☐	☐
f	The wolves kill and eat the dogs.	☐	☐
g	Bill kills the wolves with his gun.	☐	☐
h	Henry waits for three days and three nights for help to come.	☐	☐

WORD WORK

1 Match the words in the fish with the pictures.

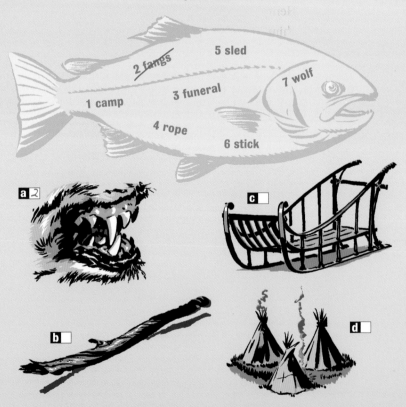

2 fangs
5 sled
1 camp
3 funeral
7 wolf
4 rope
6 stick

a ⒉
c ☐
b ☐
d ☐

Complete the sentences with new words from Chapter 1.

a The ...._land_........ in the story is the Arctic.

b The dead man in the box is a ....

c Bill and Henry .... the dogs together at night to stop them running away.

d When Bill hits the wolf on the nose it cries in ....

e Henry gives a .... to get Bill to look behind him.

f Henry and Bill see .... eyes looking at them at night.

GUESS WHAT

What happens in the next chapter? Tick four sentences.

a ☐ We learn more about the red she-wolf.
b ☐ We learn more about Lord Alfred.
c ☐ We learn more about Henry.
d ☐ We see life in the Arctic through a wolf's eyes.
e ☐ We read about hungry wolves killing different animals to live.
f ☐ We read about men killing wolves.
g ☐ A young wolf is born and learns to live in the wild.

Chapter 2
One Eye

The red she-wolf was the first to run away from the man near the fire. Then the rest of the **pack** followed. A large young grey wolf ran at the front, next to the she-wolf, and an old wolf with only one eye ran on the other side of her. Both of them wanted to make the red she-wolf their **mate**, and they showed their teeth and growled at one another.

The hungry pack ran for the rest of that day, and all through the night. And they were still running across that dead, white world the next day. Then they found the **moose**.

It was a large animal, and it was alone. Here was meat and life!

The fight began immediately, and it was wild and terrible. Fangs **bit** into the legs and sides of the moose. But the large animal killed four of the wolves, breaking open their heads with his great feet. At last he fell to the ground, and the she-wolf bit into his neck. The other wolves were quick to follow. They started to pull his body open and eat him before he was fully dead.

Their stomachs full, the pack rested and slept for the rest of that day. Next morning, the she-wolf, the young grey wolf, and One Eye took half the pack down to the Mackenzie River and across the country to the east. But slowly, in he-wolf and she-wolf pairs, the wolves went their different ways. In the end the red she-wolf was alone with the two wolves who wanted her.

The fight happened soon after. It was fast, and to the death. The younger wolf was stronger, but old One Eye was cleverer and he was soon the winner. The she-wolf sat and watched the fight. She was happy for One Eye to be the father of her **cubs**.

pack a group of wolves

mate an animal's wife or husband

moose a large plant-eating animal that lives in North America

bite (*past* **bit, bitten**) to cut something with your teeth

cub a baby wolf (or other meat-eating animal)

8

After that day, One Eye and the red wolf ran side by side, like good friends. They **hunted** and killed, and ate their meat together. They travelled across country until they came back to the Mackenzie River again.

When April came, the she-wolf looked for a place to have her cubs. She was getting very heavy, and had to run slowly. Then she found a narrow **cave**.

She looked round it carefully before sitting down to rest inside it. One Eye looked in at her, and then lay across the front of the cave. He was tired, and he slept for a time. He was hungry, too, but his mate was too tired to hunt with him. So he went out under the warm April sun alone.

He came back eight hours later, hungrier than when he went out. He stopped outside the cave. Soft, strange sounds came from inside, and they were not the sounds of his mate. When he looked in, he saw five small cubs with their mother. He tried to go into the cave, but the she-wolf growled and showed her teeth, so he went away again.

hunt to look for animals to kill and eat

cave a big hole in the ground

Four of the cubs had red hair like the she-wolf, but one was grey, like One Eye. This cub was also the strongest, but like most animals in the wild he soon learned what being very hungry was like.

Every day One Eye went out to hunt, but there were no animals and there was no meat for him to bring back to the cave. The cubs became weak and tired, and soon all they could do was sleep.

Only the grey cub opened his eyes again. The other four died before One Eye could find food.

It was soon after this that the old wolf died fighting a **lynx**. Later the she-wolf went hunting for meat and she found old One Eye's body near the lynx's cave. She did not go into the cave. The mother-lynx was inside with her cubs, and was too dangerous to fight.

One day while the she-wolf was out hunting, the grey wolf cub went to the mouth of the cave. He looked out at the world for the first time. The light was very bright, but he saw the trees and the river. He saw the mountain and the sky above it.

At first he was afraid, and the hairs on his back stood up. But nothing happened, and after a time he moved outside – and immediately fell half a metre down to the ground below! He hit his nose on the ground and cried out. Then he fell down a hill. Over and over he went until at last he stopped.

For a minute or two the grey cub was afraid to move. He sat and looked around him. Then he got up and began walking. He walked into things or fell over them, and he hurt his feet on stones and his head on trees.

lynx a big wild cat that lives in North America

stream a small river

weasel a long, thin, small meat-eating animal

He came to a **stream** and looked into the water. But when he put his foot on it, it was cold and his foot went through it! Then he heard a cry and saw a small yellow animal under his foot. It was a young **weasel**.

The weasel tried to run away but the little grey cub turned

it over with his **paw**. Suddenly, the mother-weasel came to help her child. She **attacked**, and the cub felt her teeth on his neck! He tried to pull away, but the mother-weasel was very strong. She held on to him. Blood came from the cub's neck. He started to feel very ill.

Then there was a noise and the she-wolf came running from the trees. At once the weasel left the cub to attack the she-wolf.

It was a big mistake.

The she-wolf was much stronger than the weasel, and a minute later the mother-weasel lay dead on the ground.

The little grey cub ran to his mother and she cleaned the blood from his neck with her mouth. Then the two of them ate the dead weasel before they went back to the cave to sleep.

paw the foot of an animal, for example a dog, cat or wolf

attack to start fighting

READING CHECK

Put these sentences in the correct order. Number them 1–10.

a ☐ The mother weasel starts fighting the young wolf.

b ☐ All the wolves get into pairs.

c ☐ The wolves kill a moose and eat it.

d ☐ The old wolf with one eye fights the younger grey wolf.

e ☐ Four of the baby wolves – the red ones – die.

f ☐ The red she-wolf has five babies.

g ☑ An old wolf with one eye and a younger grey wolf become friendly with the red she-wolf.

h ☐ The old wolf with one eye dies fighting a lynx.

i ☐ The mother wolf kills the mother weasel.

j ☐ The young grey wolf plays with a young weasel.

WORD WORK

1 These words don't match the pictures. Correct them.

a a ~~moose~~
a weasel

d a pack of wolves
....

b a weasel
....

e a wolf's paw
....

c a stream
....

f a wolf cub
....

Use the words from the tree to complete the sentences.

a The wolves ....*bit*........ the legs of the moose.

b The red wolf was happy to be One Eye's ....

c Wolves usually .... and kill animals together.

d The mother weasel .... the grey wolf cub to stop it hurting the young weasel.

e Wolves and dogs .... when they are angry.

> growl
> mate
> bit
> hunt
> attacked

GUESS WHAT

What happens in the next chapter?
Write *yes*, *no*, or *perhaps* for each picture.

a ....

b ....

c ....

d ....

Chapter 3
White Fang

The world outside the cave was full of surprises for the little grey cub, but his world with his mother was a happy one.

Then one morning the cub woke up and left the cave to run down to the stream for a drink. He was still half asleep after a night out hunting for meat.

Suddenly, he saw five strange 'animals' sitting under the trees. They did not jump up or show their teeth, and they did not growl. They sat silently watching him, and he felt very small and weak.

The five men were **Indians**.

One of the Indians got up and walked across to the cub. He put out his hand, and the cub growled and showed his fangs.

The Indian laughed. 'Look!' he said. 'White fangs!'

The other Indians laughed loudly. 'Bring him here!' they said.

The first man put his hand near the cub again – and the cub moved quickly to bite it. Immediately the Indian hit the cub on the head and knocked him to the ground.

The four other Indians started to laugh again, but they stopped when they heard a noise. The cub heard it, too. It was his mother coming.

The angry she-wolf ran into the middle of the little group and growled loudly. The men quickly moved away from the cub.

Then one of them looked at the she-wolf in surprise. '**Kiche**!' he called.

Indian a person who lived in North America before white people arrived

Kiche /ˈkɪtʃeɪ/

The she-wolf stopped growling and a strange light came into her eyes.

'Kiche!' the man said again. And now the she-wolf became quiet and lay down on her stomach.

The cub did not understand. He was surprised to see the Indian put his hand on the she-wolf's head, and even more surprised when she didn't bite him. After this, the other men came across and touched the she-wolf and spoke to her.

'Her father was a wolf, but her mother was a dog,' one of the Indians said. 'Do you remember, Three Eagles?'

'Yes, Grey Beaver,' a second man said. 'She ran away a year ago.'

'Yes. Because there was no food for the dogs,' Grey Beaver said. 'And since then she has lived with the wolves.'

He put his hand on the cub, and the cub growled and showed his fangs. Grey Beaver immediately hit him on the nose and the cub closed his mouth. Then the Indian **rubbed** the cub's head between the ears, and up and down his back.

'His father was a wolf,' Grey Beaver said. 'This cub is more wolf than dog. His fangs are white, so his name will be White Fang. He is my dog because Kiche was my brother's dog, and my brother is dead.'

rub to move your open hand one way and another on something

15

Grey Beaver tied Kiche to a small tree. White Fang watched him, then went and lay down beside his mother. After a time, more man-animals arrived. There were about forty men, women and children, and everyone was carrying something. There were dogs and young **puppies**, too, and these dogs carried heavy bags on their backs. They saw the wolf cub and ran and jumped on him, but the Indians **chased** them away.

White Fang learned something from this. These man-animals did not bite or fight, but they had **power** over other animals.

The group of Indians started to move away, and a small boy took Kiche and walked with her. White Fang followed them, worried about this new adventure.

They walked along beside the stream until it met the Mackenzie River. Here the Indians made their camp. White Fang watched. For him, it was all new and interesting. He moved away from his mother to look around.

After a minute or two, a puppy came up to him. The dog's name was Lip-lip, and he liked to fight. White Fang was ready to be friendly until Lip-lip showed his teeth. Then, suddenly, the young dog jumped at White Fang and bit him, three or four times. White Fang ran to his mother, crying.

To White Fang, the man-animals were like **gods**. When they walked, he got out of their way. When they called, he came.

One day, Three Eagles got ready to go on a journey up the Mackenzie River, and Grey Beaver gave him Kiche to take with him. White Fang watched Three Eagles take his mother on to a **canoe**. He jumped into the water and started to swim after them.

'Come back!' Grey Beaver shouted to him.

The Indian got into his canoe and went after the cub. It did not take him long to catch White Fang and pull him out

puppy a young dog

chase to run after something

power being able to make somebody or something do what you want

god an important 'person' who never dies and decides what happens in the world

canoe an Indian's long narrow boat

of the water. Holding him
above the boat, Grey Beaver hit him hard.
At first White Fang was surprised, then he was
angry. He growled and showed his teeth, but Grey
Beaver hit the cub harder and threw him into the bottom
of the boat.

White Fang waited only a second or two before biting the
Indian's foot. It was a big mistake. Now Grey Beaver was
even angrier. He hit the cub again and again, with his hand
and with the **paddle** of his canoe, until White Fang was
too hurt and afraid to bite him.

He followed Grey Beaver to his **tepee**. That night, he
remembered his mother and cried loudly. Grey Beaver woke
up and hit him. After that, the cub only cried quietly when
the gods were near him.

paddle a flat
piece of wood that
you use to make
a canoe move
through the water

tepee an Indian's
home

ACTIVITIES

READING CHECK

Match the first and second parts of these sentences.

1 The young grey wolf . . .
2 The red wolf comes . . .
3 She is afraid of . . .
4 Before living in the wild . . .
5 They gave her the name . . .
6 The grey wolf gets the name . . .
7 The Indians take Kiche and White Fang . . .
8 Later Three Eagles takes Kiche . . .

a because her son is in danger.
b the Indians and doesn't attack them.
c sees five Indians.
d away in a boat.
e White Fang because of his white teeth.
f to their camp.
g Kiche.
h she lived with the Indians.

WORD WORK

Correct the mistakes in these sentences. All the words come from Chapter 3.

a Our dog was a **poppy** when we got him. ....puppy....

b Grey Beaver **robbed** the grey wolf's head and back. ....

c White Fang thinks the Indians are **gots**. ....

d The Indians use **canons** to travel up and down rivers. ....

e They use **puddles** to make their boats go faster. ....

f In the summer the Indians live in camps of **topees**. ....

g White Fang sees the Indians have **flower** over other animals. ....

h The Indians **phased** away the dogs when they came to attack White Fang. ....

GUESS WHAT

What happens in the next chapter? Tick four pictures.

a ☐ The Indians move their camp.

b ☐ White Fang kills Grey Beaver.

c ☐ White Fang runs away.

d ☐ A boy hits White Fang and the wolf bites his hand.

e ☐ White Fang helps Grey Beaver's son.

f ☐ Grey Beaver hits White Fang.

Chapter 4
Learning Lessons

There was always something interesting happening in the camp and White Fang was quick to learn.

Most of all, he learned how to fight.

His worst enemy was Lip-lip. White Fang was **brave**, but Lip-lip was bigger and stronger, and was always looking for a fight. The other dogs were unfriendly, too. They **joined** Lip-lip and started fights with the little wolf cub. And when it was time to eat, they chased him away. So White Fang learned how to fight harder and faster, and to hurt others quickly. He learned how to steal their food. And he became braver and angrier and more dangerous every day.

In the autumn of the year, the Indians took down their tepees, packed their bags and got their canoes ready to go hunting.

White Fang watched some of the canoes go down the river. He understood what was happening and quickly decided not to go with them. Now he could be free!

When nobody was looking, he ran through the trees and into a stream. The water was very cold, but he wanted to hide his **trail**. After some time, he climbed out of the stream and found a place in the **undergrowth** to lie down and sleep.

Later, he woke up to the sound of Grey Beaver's voice. White Fang did not move. Again and again Grey Beaver called his name, but at last everything went quiet.

For a time, White Fang played between the trees, happy to be free. Then it got dark and everything was silent. Only the trees made noises above him. He was cold, but there was no warm side of a tepee to sleep against. And he was hungry. He remembered the pieces of meat and the fish which the men threw to him in the camp.

White Fang ran back to the Indian village, but there was

brave not afraid of doing dangerous things

join to go with

trail the smell and marks an animal's feet leave on the ground

undergrowth plants that grow under trees

20

nobody there. Suddenly, he felt lonely and afraid.

The next morning he started to run along the river **bank**. He ran all day without resting. He climbed mountains and swam across streams, always following the big river. It started to snow, but he ran all that night and again the next day. By now he was weak and hungry.

When he was nearly too tired to stand up, he heard the sounds of the camp. Then, near the river bank he saw the fire! And he could smell food cooking!

Grey Beaver sat next to the fire. He looked up and saw the little grey cub. White Fang **crawled** slowly across to the Indian. He lay down beside him and waited for Grey Beaver to hit him or shout at him. But Grey Beaver did not hit him, he gave White Fang some meat. White Fang smelled it carefully, then started to eat. He was not afraid now. He was warm, and happy to be back with the gods.

bank the ground at the side of a river

crawl to move along slowly with the body close to the ground

When it was the middle of December, Grey Beaver went on a journey up the Mackenzie River. His son, Mit-sah, and his wife, Kloo-kooch, went with him. They took two sleds. Grey Beaver was driving the bigger sled, and Mit-sah was driving the smaller sled. White Fang was only eight months old, and Grey Beaver tied him to Mit-sah's sled. Lip-lip ran at the front, with White Fang and five other puppies behind him.

White Fang learned to be afraid of men's hands. It was true that they sometimes threw him meat, but more often they threw sticks at him or hurt him. And in the village of Great Slave **Lake**, White Fang learned a new lesson. A boy was cutting up some meat when some of it fell on the ground near White Fang. Meat that fell on the ground was usually for the dogs, so the young wolf cub immediately started to eat it. Then he saw the boy put down his knife and **pick up** a large, heavy stick.

White Fang did not understand. He ran away, but the boy chased him and tried to hit him. White Fang became angry. Without stopping to think, he turned and bit the boy's hand.

Immediately he was sorry and afraid. He knew that it was wrong to bite the hand of a man-animal. Later, the boy and his family came to see Grey Beaver. But Grey Beaver, Kloo-kooch and Mit-sah all spoke angrily to the boy and his family.

'The boy was wrong to hit White Fang,' Grey Beaver told them. And after they went away, he did not hit the young cub.

So White Fang learned that there were *his* gods, and there were *other* gods. His gods could hit him at any time, but other gods must not hit him when he was doing nothing wrong.

Before the day was finished, White Fang learned more of this lesson about his gods and other gods.

Mit-sah was alone, getting wood for the fire. White Fang was watching him. The boy with the bitten hand, and some

lake a large piece of water with land all around it

pick up to take in your hand

of his friends, saw Mit-sah. They went after him and started to shout bad words and attack him.

At first White Fang did nothing. This was a fight between man-gods, and nothing to do with him. But then he remembered that this was Mit-sah, one of *his* gods. Angrily, he ran and chased the other boys away, biting some of them.

When Mit-sah told his story at the camp, Grey Beaver gave White Fang more meat than all the other dogs. And from this, White Fang learned that it was his job to **protect** Grey Beaver's family and **property**.

protect to fight to save something

property something that belongs to you

READING CHECK

Correct six more mistakes in the chapter summary.

Lip-lip is White Fang's greatest ~~friend~~ *enemy* and White Fang learns to fight with him. In the

summer the Indians move their camp to go hunting. White Fang runs away from them.

After some time he feels thirsty so he goes back, but the Indian camp isn't there. He goes

along by the side of a great road and in the end he finds the Indian camp in a new place.

Grey Beaver is angry to see him. In December, Grey Beaver goes on a journey with his son

and his wife. White Fang pulls a sled for them. When a boy hits White Fang for eating some

meat on the ground, White Fang bites the boy's foot. Later White Fang helps Grey Beaver's

brother when some boys begin to attack him.

WORD WORK

**Use the words in the tepee to
complete the sentences on page 25.**

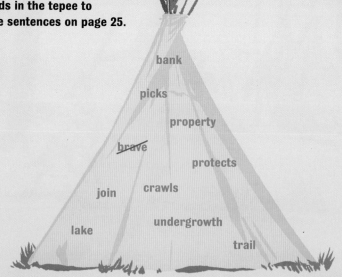

bank

picks

property

~~brave~~

protects

join   crawls

lake   undergrowth

trail

a White Fang isn't afraid of anything. He's very ....brave.... .

b He goes across a stream to stop other dogs from following his ....

c He hid under some trees, in the ....

d After some time he decides to .... the Indians again.

e He goes along a river .... and in the end he finds their new camp.

f He .... across the ground when he gets near Grey Beaver.

g The Indians make a new village near a big ....

h A boy .... up a stick to hit White Fang.

i Grey Beaver .... White Fang from the boy's family.

j The things you have – your house, your car – are your ....

GUESS WHAT

What happens in the next chapter? Tick the boxes.

	Yes	No
a All the dogs in the Indian village are friendly with White Fang.	☐	☐
b There is another time when all the animals and people in the land are hungry.	☐	☐
c White Fang runs away from the Indian village.	☐	☐
d He goes to live in a white man's house.	☐	☐
e He kills and eats a lynx.	☐	☐
f Some wolves run after him.	☐	☐
g White Fang finds it hard to run away from them.	☐	☐
h He goes back to the Indian village.	☐	☐

Chapter 5
The Famine

It was April when Grey Beaver finished his long journey and arrived at his home village. White Fang was now a year old. His coat was a wolf-grey colour, and he looked like a wolf. He was strong, and he could fight with the older dogs and win.

When White Fang first came to live with Grey Beaver, one of the oldest dogs always chased him away. That dog's name was Baseek. But things were changing now. Baseek was getting older and weaker while White Fang was getting stronger every day.

White Fang first came to know this when he was eating some moose meat alone, away from the other dogs. It was a large piece of meat on the **bone**, and Baseek wanted it. He ran to take it from between White Fang's paws. Without thinking, the wolf cub jumped on Baseek and bit his neck.

Baseek was surprised, but he growled at White Fang and suddenly saw **fear** in the young wolf cub's eyes. Braver now, Baseek walked across to the meat and started to eat it. The fear went from White Fang's eyes when he saw this. Now he was angry. It was *his* bone, not Baseek's! He jumped on the old dog and bit off his ear! Then he bit him in the neck, on the **shoulder**, and on the nose. Baseek dropped the bone and walked away with his head down.

bone a hard white thing in an animal's body

fear the feeling that you have when you are afraid

shoulder this is between your arm and your neck

The months went past and White Fang grew bigger and stronger. But he was not like the other dogs. The wolf in him made him very different and much more dangerous, and so the other dogs left him alone.

One thing made White Fang very angry. He did not like people to laugh at him. They could laugh at other things, but not at him. When they did, he became angry and very dangerous, and the other dogs ran away from him.

When he was three years old, there was another **famine**.
There were no wild animals to kill, and no fish in the rivers
or lakes. It was a terrible time, when only the strong
survived. The older and weaker Indians in the village began
to die, and the children cried because they were hungry. The
women left the little food there was for the men. They went
out to hunt, looking everywhere for animal trails, but they
came home with little or no meat. Dogs began to eat other
dogs, and the Indians started to eat their animals.

famine a time
when there is not
enough food in a
country

survive to live
through a difficult
and dangerous time

During this time, White Fang left the camp and went to live in the **woods**. He could run faster and was a better hunter than the other dogs. He could catch the animals that were too small or too quick for the Indian hunters to kill. Because of this, he did not die when others were dying.

One day he saw a young wolf in the woods. The wolf was thin and weak, but for a short time White Fang thought about going with him. He thought about joining his wild brothers in the wolf pack. But his stomach was empty and he was too hungry to think for long. After a minute, he killed the young wolf and ate him.

Another day, ten or twelve wolves saw him and chased him. But White Fang's luck was with him. That morning he was feeling strong after killing and eating a lynx. So he could run faster than the weak and hungry wolves, and he got away from them without any trouble.

In the last days of the famine, White Fang met Lip-lip. Each animal was surprised to see the other, and they both growled and got ready to attack. Lip-lip was also living in the woods at that time. But he was not a good hunter like

woods a place where lots of trees grow together

White Fang, so he was not as strong. Because of this, the fight didn't **last** long.

White Fang attacked fast and hard. He threw Lip-lip to the ground and began to bite into his neck. Lip-lip was too weak to fight back, and he died quickly. White Fang looked at him for a minute or two, then he walked away.

One day, not long after this, White Fang looked out from the woods and saw a **clearing**. The clearing was near the Mackenzie River, and he saw the tepees and fires of an Indian village there.

White Fang looked down on it. After a time, he **recognized** some of the sounds, and some of the faces. It was the old village, but it was now in a new place. He also recognized the smell of fish cooking, so he knew that there was food to eat.

White Fang came out from the trees and **trotted** into the village. He soon found Grey Beaver's tepee and went inside. Grey Beaver was not there, but Kloo-kooch was happy to see him and gave him some fish. Then White Fang lay down to wait for Grey Beaver.

last to continue for a time

clearing an open place in the middle of woods

recognize to see something and know what it is

trot to run with short, quick steps

READING CHECK

Correct the mistakes in these sentences.

a White Fang fights Baseek and ~~loses.~~ *wins*

b When White Fang is four, all the animals and people in the land are hungry.

c The women leave their food for the children in the village.

d White Fang goes to live in the town.

e He kills and eats a thin, weak old wolf.

f Fourteen wolves run after him but he escapes.

g Lip-lip runs away at the end of a fight with White Fang.

h When White Fang goes back to the Indian village, Grey Beaver gives him some fish.

WORD WORK

Find the words in the Indian shoes to complete the sentences.

a White Fang likes eating meat on the b o n e .

b At first White Fang is afraid and Baseek can see the f _ _ _ in his eyes.

c Then White Fang bites Baseek on the neck and the s _ _ _ _ _ _ _ .

d When White Fang is three, there is f _ _ _ _ _ in the land and all the animals are hungry.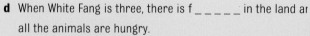

e Many animals die but White Fang s _ _ _ _ _ _ _ because he is very strong.

f He goes to live far from the Indian village in the w _ _ _ _ .

g The famine l _ _ _ _ for many months.

h White Fang sees an Indian village in a c _ _ _ _ _ _ _ between the trees.

i He r _ _ _ _ _ _ _ _ _ the sounds and smells of the village.

j Happily he t _ _ _ _ into the village and goes to Grey Beaver's tepee to eat some fish.

GUESS WHAT

What happens in the next chapter? Tick the boxes.

a Why does Grey Beaver go to Fort Yukon?
   1 ☐ To sell clothes and shoes there.
   2 ☐ To buy clothes there.
   3 ☐ To sell horses there.

b What does White Fang do in Fort Yukon?
   1 ☐ He fights with white men's dogs.
   2 ☐ He runs away from Grey Beaver.
   3 ☐ He kills a man.

c What happens to Grey Beaver?
   1 ☐ He makes lots of money.
   2 ☐ He buys a house.
   3 ☐ He kills a man.

d What does the white man do?
   1 ☐ He sees Grey Beaver fighting.
   2 ☐ He tries to buy White Fang.
   3 ☐ He gives a dog to Grey Beaver.

Chapter 6
Beauty Smith

When White Fang was nearly five years old, Grey Beaver took him on another great journey. They went down the Mackenzie River, and across the Rocky Mountains to the Yukon River. When they stopped at villages, White Fang was quick to fight with the dogs there. They did not recognize the **fact** that he was part wolf, and they were not ready for his fast and dangerous attacks. Many of them died in these **deadly** fights.

fact something that is true

deadly ending in death

White Fang and Grey Beaver arrived at Fort Yukon in the summer of 1898. At this time, thousands of men were going up the Yukon River to Dawson City and the Klondike to look for gold. Grey Beaver knew about this. He had clothes and shoes made from animal skins with him to sell to these people.

In Fort Yukon, White Fang saw white men for the first time. To begin with he did not go near these strange new gods. But he felt sure that they were different. They had more power than the Indians he knew. They too were interested in him, and what was more they did not hurt the dogs who went near them.

Only a few white men lived in Fort Yukon, but a **steamer** arrived every two or three days. It stopped for five or six hours, and then went away again. Many more white men came and went on the steamer.

There was no work for White Fang to do. Grey Beaver was busy selling things to the white men and getting rich. So White Fang spent his time starting fights with the white men's dogs. None of them could fight well. They made a lot of noise and ran and jumped at White Fang, but he threw them off or bit them. Then he left them for the other Indian dogs to kill. This was the right thing to do because the white gods were always angry when their dogs died in a fight. When it happened, the men chased the Indian dogs and hit them with heavy sticks while White Fang watched.

He enjoyed the fights and they were easy to start. When the dogs came off the steamer and saw him, they immediately recognized a wild and dangerous animal. And because, soon after they were born, they learned to kill wild things, they attacked him.

The white men in Fort Yukon did not like the gold-hunters who came off the steamer, but they liked to take their money. And they were always happy to see the white men's dogs chased and killed by the Indian dogs.

One man liked the fights more than any of the others. As soon as he heard a steamer coming, he ran down to the **dock** to meet it. His name was Smith. Nobody knew his first name, but the men in the town called him 'Beauty' because he was *not* beautiful. He was a small man with large yellow eyes and big yellow teeth like fangs. He did the cooking and washed the dishes for the other men, but they did not like him. He was a **coward**, and like many cowards, he was a **cruel** man, too.

Beauty Smith watched White Fang fighting, and he wanted to buy the wolf-dog. He tried to make a friend of the animal,

steamer a ship

dock the place where a ship stops

coward a person who is often afraid

cruel hard, and wanting to hurt other people

but White Fang growled at him and showed him his teeth.
He did not like this man.

White Fang was in Grey Beaver's camp when Beauty Smith
first visited it. He watched the two men talking together for
a long time. The Indian did not want to sell White Fang. He
was rich and did not need the money.

But Beauty Smith visited Grey Beaver's camp often, and
there were always one or two bottles of whiskey under his
coat. Grey Beaver liked the whiskey, and soon more and more

of his money went on it. After a short time, he had no money **left**. Then Beauty Smith spoke to him again about White Fang, and **persuaded** Grey Beaver to sell the dog to him for more of the bottles.

'You catch him,' said the Indian, 'and you can have him.'

After two days, Beauty Smith went back to Grey Beaver. '*You* catch him,' he said.

White Fang trotted into the camp that evening and Grey Beaver tied a long thin piece of **leather** to him. The Indian sat down with a bottle of whiskey and drank for an hour before Beauty Smith arrived. The white man stood above White Fang and put out a hand to rub the animal's head. White Fang tried to bite it, and Grey Beaver hit him on the head.

Beauty Smith was angry and afraid. He went away and came back with a big stick. White Fang jumped at him, but the man hit him hard with the stick. White Fang fell down

left there after all the rest has gone

persuade to make somebody change their way of thinking by speaking to them

leather animal skin

on the ground and the man took the leather and pulled it. Now White Fang followed him.

At his home, Beauty Smith tied White Fang to a door with the leather and went to bed. White Fang waited an hour. Then he started to bite the leather. After a minute he was free, and he went back to Grey Beaver's camp.

In the morning, Grey Beaver took him back to Beauty Smith. The white man hit White Fang hard, then tied him with a thick rope. After many hours, the dog bit through the rope and ran back to Grey Beaver.

The next morning, Beauty Smith came for him once more. He hit the animal again and again, until White Fang was weak and **sick**.

Grey Beaver watched but said nothing. White Fang was not his property now. And it was time for him to leave Fort Yukon and start his journey home.

sick ill

READING CHECK

Match the sentences with the people.

Grey Beaver

Beauty Smith

a ... goes to Fort Yukon city to
sell things there.

b ... has a job cooking and
washing dishes in Fort Yukon.

c ... is very ugly.

d ... wants to buy White Fang.

e ... brings Grey Beaver whiskey to
drink.

f ... spends all his money on whiskey

g ... buys White Fang.

h ... hits White Fang with a stick and
takes him away.

i ... leaves Fort Yukon without White
Fang.

WORD WORK

Find the words in the rope to complete the sentences on page 39.

cowardcrueldeadlydockfactleatherleftpersuadessicksteame

ACTIVITIES

a It's a f a c t that White Fang's father was a wolf.

b He likes having _ _ _ _ _ _ fights with other dogs.

c White men come up the river to Fork Yukon on a _ _ _ _ _ _ _ _ .

d They get off the boat at the Fort Yukon _ _ _ _ .

e Beauty Smith isn't a brave man; he's a _ _ _ _ _ _ _ .

f Grey Beaver sells lots of soft _ _ _ _ _ _ _ clothes and shoes in Fort Yukon.

g Grey Beaver spends lots of money on whiskey and in the end he has no money _ _ _ _ .

h Smith _ _ _ _ _ _ _ _ _ Grey Beaver to sell White Fang to him for some more whiskey.

i Smith is a _ _ _ _ _ man. He doesn't feel sorry for anyone.

j When Smith hits White Fang with a stick, the wolf feels weak and _ _ _ _ .

GUESS WHAT

What happens in the next chapter? Tick the boxes.

	Yes	Perhaps	No
a Beauty Smith is very nice to White Fang.	☐	☐	☐
b White Fang fights and kills many dogs.	☐	☐	☐
c Smith makes no money from these dog fights.	☐	☐	☐
d One day White Fang has to fight a moose.	☐	☐	☐
e He always wins the fights he is in.	☐	☐	☐
f People call White Fang 'The Fighting Wolf'. He is famous.	☐	☐	☐
g One day White Fang loses a fight with another dog.	☐	☐	☐
h White Fang nearly dies. It is the end of his fighting days.	☐	☐	☐
i Grey Beaver comes to take White Fang back to the Indian village.	☐	☐	☐

Chapter 7
Cherokee

White Fang **hated** Beauty Smith more than anyone. The little man did everything he could think of to make White Fang angry. He hurt him and he laughed at him. He did this because he knew that angry dogs were the best fighters, and Smith wanted a good fighting dog.

He kept White Fang in a **pen**, and one day, a group of men came to look at him. White Fang ran round the inside of the pen, growling and jumping up at them. Then the door of the pen opened and Beauty Smith pushed a big dog inside.

White Fang immediately jumped on the dog and bit it. Blood came from the dog's neck, but it growled and tried to catch White Fang. The wolf was too fast for him. He turned and jumped, and bit the dog's ears and face. There was more blood.

The men **cheered** and whistled when White Fang killed the dog. After a minute, Smith went into the pen with a big stick

hate the opposite of love

pen a small open space with walls around it to put animals in

cheer to shout to show that you are pleased

and knocked White Fang away from the dead animal before pulling it outside. Then the men began to pay him money for their **bets**.

White Fang was a prisoner in his pen. He could not hunt or pull a sled, but he enjoyed the cruel and deadly fights. And Smith enjoyed taking money from the men who came to watch them.

When the first of the snow fell, Beauty Smith took White Fang on a steamer up the Yukon River to Dawson City. There were always men round his **cage** on the steamer. They pushed sticks into the cage to make him growl and jump at them, then they laughed at him. This made him even angrier.

When the steamer arrived at Dawson, Smith kept White Fang in the cage. Men paid half a dollar in gold to see 'The Fighting Wolf'. When White Fang tried to sleep, they pushed sticks into the cage to wake him up.

Some nights, Beauty Smith took him into the woods outside the town. When it was morning, a lot of men arrived. Always, one or more of them came with dogs for White Fang to fight. Usually he killed the dogs, or he chased and bit them until they were too weak to fight any more. He knew more about fighting than they did, and he was too fast and too clever for them.

Then there was a fight with a lynx, and White Fang nearly died. After the lynx, there were no more animals left who could fight him.

Until the spring. And a dog called Cherokee.

Cherokee was a strange dog. He was short and heavy, and he belonged to a man called Tim Keenan.

'Go to him, Cherokee!' the men shouted. 'Eat the Fighting Wolf!'

Cherokee did not move. He was not afraid, he was lazy.

bet when you put money on a fighter, saying that he will win; if you are right you win money, if you are wrong you lose it

cage an open box to put dangerous animals in

41

Then Tim Keenan put a hand on Cherokee's back and began to rub him there. This made Cherokee angry, and he started to growl. The growling got louder and louder, and it made White Fang growl.

Keenan pushed Cherokee, and the dog began to run. Immediately, White Fang jumped on him and bit the back of his neck. Blood came from behind Cherokee's ear, but he made no sound. He turned and followed White Fang.

Again and again White Fang jumped on Cherokee and bit him. Now there was blood on the dog's face, but he did not cry out with pain. Again and again Cherokee turned and followed the wolf. He did not hurry. White Fang tried to knock Cherokee to the ground, but Cherokee was too short and heavy.

Then the dog turned his head to look at the men. White Fang ran at him and tried to push him to the ground. But this time he moved too quickly and pushed too hard. He went over Cherokee's back and **crashed** to the ground, his paws **in the air**!

He got back on his feet quickly, but Cherokee attacked! He bit White Fang hard, and his teeth stayed in the wolf's neck. White Fang ran wildly round and round, but the dog's teeth stayed in his neck and it was **bleeding**.

White Fang stopped when he was too tired to run any more. At first he lay on his side, but Cherokee pushed him on to his back and sat on top of him. The dog's teeth were still in White Fang's neck, and the wolf was getting weaker and weaker from **loss** of blood.

The men with bets on Cherokee cheered loudly. Then Beauty Smith pushed through them and started laughing at White Fang. White Fang went wild with anger. He pulled himself up on to his feet and began to move round inside the circle of men. Round and round he went, falling and getting up on to his feet again. But soon he was too weak to get up any more.

Then Beauty Smith ran to White Fang and began to kick him.

Suddenly, a tall young man pushed through the people. 'You coward!' he shouted, and then he **punched** Beauty Smith in the face. Smith fell to the ground. Next, the young man turned and called to a friend, 'Matt, come and help me.'

Another man came across, and they tried to pull Cherokee off White Fang. But the dog's teeth stayed in White Fang's neck.

'We've got to get his mouth open, Mr Scott,' Matt said.

He took a gun from his coat and put it between the dog's teeth. Using the gun as a **lever**, he opened Cherokee's mouth.

crash to fall noisily

in the air not on the ground

bleed (*past* **bled**) to lose blood

loss when you lose something

punch to hit with your closed hand

lever a stick that you use to open something

At the same time, Weedon Scott carefully pulled White Fang's neck out.

'Take your dog!' Matt told Tim Keenan.

Keenan moved quickly to get his dog, and took him away.

White Fang tried to get up on his feet, but he was too weak. He lay in the snow with his eyes half-shut.

'Matt, how much does a good sled-dog cost?' Scott asked.

'Three hundred dollars,' Matt answered.

'And how much for this one now, after the fight?' Scott asked.

'Half of that,' Matt said.

Scott turned to Beauty Smith, who was on his feet again. 'Did you hear that?' he said. 'I'm going to take your dog, and I'm going to give you a hundred and fifty dollars for him.'

'I'm not selling him,' Smith said.

'Oh yes, you are!' Weedon Scott said. 'Here's the money. Take it, or I'll punch you again.'

After a minute, Scott finally persuaded Smith to take the money, and then he walked away.

When White Fang was strong again, there was no pen to keep him a prisoner. At first he was afraid of Weedon Scott and Matt. When Scott tried to be friendly, White Fang bit his hand, then waited for the man-god to hurt him. But nothing happened. The next day, Scott came with a piece of meat, which he threw on the ground. White Fang smelled the meat, but looked at Scott. After a minute he ate the meat.

The man-god talked to him in a quiet, kind voice. Then he put his hand on White Fang's head and rubbed it. This was something new and strange to White Fang. But he liked it, and it was the beginning of a new life for him.

In the spring, Scott went away. White Fang waited all night

for him outside the house. Days came and went, but Scott did not come. White Fang **pined** for the first time in his life.

Matt wrote to Weedon Scott: *The wolf won't pull a sled and he won't eat. He wants to know where you are, but how can I tell him? I think he's going to die.*

And then, one night, White Fang made a soft **whining** sound and looked up at the door. Seconds later, the door opened and Scott came in. He saw White Fang and called him. The wolf came quickly, and there was a strange light in his eyes. Scott rubbed White Fang's head and ears. The wolf growled happily. For the first time in his life, he felt a very strong love for someone.

pine to become sick because someone that you love is not there

whine to cry in a high voice

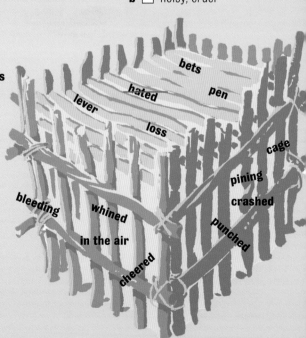

READING CHECK

Choose the right words to finish the sentences.

1 Beauty Smith does everything to make White Fang .... him.
   a ☐ like
   b ☑ hate

2 White Fang .... fighting other dogs.
   a ☐ loves
   b ☐ doesn't like

3 Smith .... making money with White Fang.
   a ☐ doesn't mind
   b ☐ enjoys

4 Cherokee is a .... fighter.
   a ☐ slow but deadly
   b ☐ fast and deadly

5 Weedon Scott pays Smith .... for White Fang.
   a ☐ 300 dollars
   b ☐ 150 dollars

6 Weedon Scott talks to White Fang in a .... voice.
   a ☐ quiet, kind
   b ☐ noisy, cruel

WORD WORK

Use the words in the cage to complete Weedon Scott's diary on page 47.

bets

hated

pen

lever

loss

cage

pining

crashed

bleeding

whined

punched

in the air

cheered

Before I got him, the Fighting Wolf lived with Beauty Smith. I'm sure he **a)** <u>hated</u> him, Smith was so bad to him. The Wolf lived in a **(b)** _ _ _ and he travelled in a **(c)** _ _ _ _ .

People loved watching the Wolf fight, and they opened their mouths and **(d)** _ _ _ _ _ _ _ _ when he won. And Beauty Smith loved taking their **(e)** _ _ _ _ . I'm sure he made a lot of money with every fight.

I saw the end of the fight between the Wolf and the dog Cherokee. The Wolf **(f)** _ _ _ _ _ _ _ _ to the ground. His legs were **(g)** _ _ _ _ _ _ _ _ and his neck - with Cherokee's teeth in it - was **(h)** _ _ _ _ _ _ _ _ a lot. He was weak from **(i)** _ _ _ _ of blood.

I was angry so I **(j)** _ _ _ _ _ _ _ _ Smith in the face. Then my friend Matt used his gun as a **(k)** _ _ _ _ _ _ to open Cherokee's mouth.

I bought the Wolf from Smith and tried to teach him to love me. I left Fort Yukon in the spring and after a short time Matt wrote to say: 'Weedon, the wolf is **(l)** _ _ _ _ _ _ for you.' And when I went back to visit, the Wolf **(m)** _ _ _ _ _ _ _ when I got near the house.'

GUESS WHAT

What happens in the next chapter?
Match the first and second parts of these sentences.

a Weedon Scott
b White Fang
c Scott takes White Fang
d California
e Scott's family
f In the end they

1 decides to go with Scott on the streamer.
2 leaves White Fang with Matt again.
3 is strange for White Fang.
4 love white Fang.
5 to his family home in California.
6 are afraid of White Fang when he arrives.

Chapter 8
California

'Listen to that!' Matt said at supper one night.

Scott listened. A **low**, sad whining noise came through the door.

'That wolf knows that you're leaving,' Matt said.

'I can't take a wolf to California,' Scott replied.

Next day, two Indians took Scott's bags to the dock. Scott came to the door of the house and called White Fang inside.

'I can't take you with me,' he said, and he rubbed White Fang's ears. 'Now give me a growl and say goodbye.'

White Fang did not growl. He pushed his head between Scott's arm and body. The sound of the steamer came from the river.

'It's time to go,' Matt said.

The two men shut the doors of the house and went down to the dock. From the house came the noise of White Fang whining.

low soft and quiet

'Write and tell me about him,' Scott told Matt.

Some minutes later, Scott went onto the steamer and the two men said goodbye. Suddenly, Matt saw White Fang on the boat, behind Scott! There were cuts and blood on the wolf's face.

'Well, look at that! He jumped through the window to be with you!' Matt said.

Scott did not answer. He was thinking quickly.

'Goodbye, Matt,' he said, after a minute. 'About the wolf – you don't need to write. *I'll* write to *you* about him.'

Scott got off the steamer at San Francisco. The noise of the city made White Fang shake with fear, and he stayed very near to Scott. A train took them out into the country. When they got off, a **carriage** was waiting for them. A man and a woman came across to Scott. The woman put her arms round Scott's neck.

When White Fang saw this, he growled, the hairs on his back **bristled** and he **sprang** at her. Scott pulled him away and said, 'It's all right, mother. He'll soon learn.' He looked at White Fang. 'Down!' he said. White Fang lay down on the ground. Scott opened his arms to his mother again, but watched White Fang. 'Down!' he said again.

White Fang watched silently, and did not move.

The two men and the woman got into the carriage and drove away. White Fang ran behind. After fifteen minutes they turned into a small road between some trees. A dog ran out of the trees between White Fang and the carriage.

White Fang started to run at the dog – and stopped. It was a she-dog. He couldn't attack her. But the dog was afraid, and she bit White Fang.

'Here, Collie!' called the strange man in the carriage.

Weedon Scott laughed. 'It's all right, father,' he said. 'White Fang will have to learn many things here in California. He can start learning now.'

carriage an old kind of car that horses pull

bristle to stand up straight

spring (*past* **sprang, sprung**) to jump

They drove on towards a large house. White Fang pushed Collie to the ground and ran after the carriage. Collie got up and chased after him, but she could not catch him. Then a large dog came from the house and knocked White Fang to the ground. The wolf got up, ready to kill it.

Collie arrived in time to knock White Fang over again, and this **delayed** the wolf, **preventing** him from attacking immediately. At once Weedon Scott held White Fang, while the other man called the two dogs to him.

'Dick! Collie!' he said. 'Come here!'

More gods came out of the house, then they all went inside and White Fang followed them.

Scott's home was called Sierra Vista. White Fang soon learned to live there. He also learned to live with the other dogs, but he was not friendly with them. He learned about Scott's family. There was Scott's father, who was a **judge**. And there was Scott's mother, his wife, his two sisters, and his two children.

The months came and went, and White Fang was happy in his new home. Only Collie made life difficult. She followed him and growled at him. Did she hate him or was she pining for him? It was hard to say.

Weedon Scott often went out on his horse, and White Fang always went with him. One day, Scott fell from the horse and broke his leg. White Fang growled at the horse, but Scott stopped him.

'Home!' he told White Fang. 'Go home!'

White Fang did not want to leave him. Scott saw this and spoke quietly. 'It's all right,' he said. 'Go home and tell them, wolf.'

The family were sitting outside the house when White Fang ran up to Judge Scott and began growling.

'Go away and lie down!' the judge said.

delay to make something go slower

prevent to stop

judge a person who decides how long criminals should go to prison for their crimes

Then White Fang turned to Scott's mother and **tugged** at her dress with his teeth. 'Something's happened to Weedon!' she said.

They all got up quickly and followed White Fang to help Scott.

After this, they all loved White Fang.

In the second winter at Sierra Vista, Collie became more friendly with White Fang. One day they ran together in the woods like White Fang's mother Kiche and old One Eye all those years before.

Around about this time, a prisoner got out of San Quentin prison. His name was Jim Hall, and he was dangerous. For days the police tried to catch him, but he was too quick and too clever for them.

tug to pull

The women in the Scott family were afraid.

'You sent Jim Hall to prison and he hates you for it,' they said to Judge Scott. 'Perhaps he'll come here to attack you.'

The judge told them not to worry. But the women were right and he was wrong.

One night, White Fang woke up and heard someone moving inside the house. He smelled a strange god and the hairs on his neck bristled. The stranger walked softly, but White Fang followed him silently to the bottom of the stairs. The stranger stopped and listened. White Fang knew that his master's bedroom was at the top of the stairs, and he knew that he had to protect his master from this stranger.

As soon as the man put a foot on the stairs, White Fang sprang! The two of them crashed to the floor, and White Fang bit the man's neck.

The family woke up to the noise of crashing furniture. Soon after this there were sounds of **gunshots**, and a man's scream. Then everything went quiet. Weedon Scott put on a light, then he and Judge Scott came downstairs with guns in their hands.

A dead man with a bleeding neck lay at the bottom of the stairs.

Judge Scott **approached** and looked at his face. 'It's Jim Hall,' he said.

White Fang was lying next to the criminal with his eyes closed, and three gunshot **wounds** in his side. He was weak from loss of blood.

gunshot the shooting of a gun

approach to get near

wound a hole in the body from a knife or a gunshot

stable a building where horses live

White Fang did not die. He survived. He slept for many long hours, for many weeks and his wounds closed. At last after some months he got up and stood on his four legs. All the family followed him outside and watched. Very slowly, White Fang walked to the **stable**. Collie lay near the stable door, and six fat puppies were crawling about and playing beside

her. White Fang looked at them, but Collie growled at him in a low voice and he did not go near them.

One of the women put an arm round Collie to prevent her from moving, then Weedon Scott picked up one of the little dogs and put it down next to White Fang. Collie watched and growled again. Then White Fang put his nose next to the puppy's nose. Weedon Scott and the family laughed and cheered. White Fang was surprised, but he lay down next to the little dog.

The rest of the puppies came and climbed over him.

Happy at last, White Fang went to sleep in the sun.

ACTIVITIES

READING CHECK

What do they say?

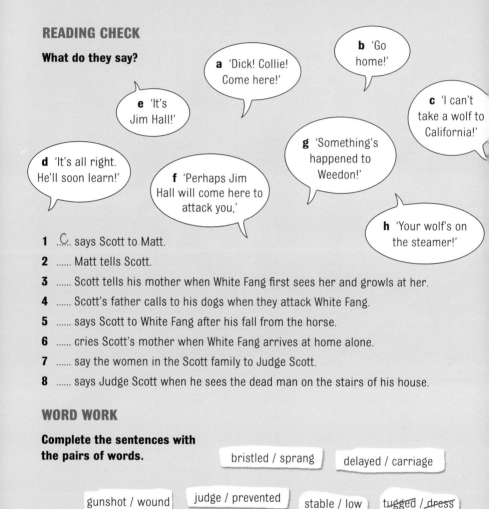

a 'Dick! Collie! Come here!'

b 'Go home!'

c 'I can't take a wolf to California!'

d 'It's all right. He'll soon learn!'

e 'It's Jim Hall!'

f 'Perhaps Jim Hall will come here to attack you,'

g 'Something's happened to Weedon!'

h 'Your wolf's on the steamer!'

1 ..C.. says Scott to Matt.

2 ...... Matt tells Scott.

3 ...... Scott tells his mother when White Fang first sees her and growls at her.

4 ...... Scott's father calls to his dogs when they attack White Fang.

5 ...... says Scott to White Fang after his fall from the horse.

6 ...... cries Scott's mother when White Fang arrives at home alone.

7 ...... say the women in the Scott family to Judge Scott.

8 ...... says Judge Scott when he sees the dead man on the stairs of his house.

WORD WORK

Complete the sentences with the pairs of words.

bristled / sprang   delayed / carriage   gunshot / wound   judge / prevented   stable / low   tugged / dress

a White Fang ..tugged.. at Mrs Scott's ..dress.. .

b The hair on the dog's back .... and then he ....

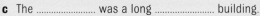
c The .... was a long .... building.

d They heard a .... and when they entered the room Max was lying on the sofa with a .... on his leg.

e The .... sat in bed feeling ill. His cold .... him from going to the party.

f The sheep on the road .... the .... and they were late!

GUESS WHAT

What happens after the story ends?

a ☐ One of White Fang's and Collie's puppies runs away to live in the wild.

b ☐ Weedon goes with his wife and children to live in New York leaving White Fang in California with his mother and father.

c ☐ Weedon takes White Fang back to Fort Yukon again because he prefers living in the wild.

d ☐ Grey Beaver sees White Fang's photograph in the newspaper and comes to see him in California.

e ☐ Beauty Smith writes his side of White Fang's story and sells it to the newspapers for lots of money.

Project A *My Pet*

1 Look at this project on pets. Match the photos with the writing.

2

4

1

3

5

Our Pets

a ☐ We have lots of goldfish in a pond in our garden. The two big fish are called Sophie and Isidoro. All the little fish are their children. They eat lots of fish-food.

b ☐ We also have a green frog in our pond. He makes a lot of noise. He hasn't got a name.

c ☐ This is our dog Roger. He's a lovely golden brown colour and a medium-sized dog. He's six years old. He's very friendly but a bit wild. He can jump over our garden wall when he wants. He likes running after cats.

d ☐ This is our dog Molly. She's got a smooth black coat. She's two years old and a small dog. She's very friendly and very silly. She jumps about and barks a lot.

e ☐ This is my snake. I call him Mambo. He eats insects and other small animals and he lives in a glass tank called a vivarium. My dad doesn't like him very much but my mum thinks he's great. His fangs aren't dangerous.

Answer these questions. You can write answers for your own pet or for an imaginary pet. Use a dictionary to help you.

What's it called?

What kind of animal is it?

c What colour is it?

d How old is it?

e How big is it?

f What are its habits?

Write about your pets. Use the pet project on page 56 to help you.

white rat   **snake**   **parrot**   **monkey**

iguana   **puppy**   **kitten**

Project B *Animal Rescue*

1 Read about this animal rescue story. Match the sentences with the pictures.

a . . . Oscar's mother died and Oscar was all alone and very hungry.
b When he was older he was taken to the Orang-utan rescue centre.
c After a time, he was found by Orang-utan rescue workers and they gave
him some food.
d Oscar the Orang-utan was born in the wild in a forest in Borneo.
e In the end Oscar left the centre and was sent back to live in the wild again.
f When men cut down all the trees in the forest to make wood, . . .

1 d

2

3 ☐

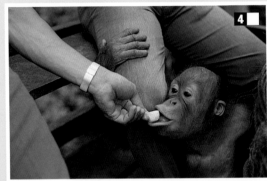

4 ☐

5 ☐

6 ☐

2 Look at the animal rescue story on page 60.

3 Write sentences for the pictures using the words in the boxes.

a Leo / lion / and / sister Leah / born / safari park / England

b when / safari park / close / Leo and Leah / sell / to / small family circus

c cage there / small and dirty / many people / worry / about / lions

ANIMAL RESCUE

d journalist / go / write / a story about them.

e rich woman / read / story / in / newspaper / and gave / money / help

f Leo and Leah / go / live / big wild animal park / Africa.

GRAMMAR CHECK

Present Perfect and Past Simple

We use the Present Perfect to talk about things happening at some time in the past without saying when.

Have you visited Fort Yukon? Yes, I have./No, I haven't.

I've seen a picture of the place. But I haven't been there.

We can also use the Present Perfect to talk about things that began in the past and that are continuing now. In this case, we often use for and since with the Present Perfect.

I've known Grey Beaver for many years. (for + a period of time)

White Fang has become friendlier since he arrived. (since = from a point in the past up to now)

We use the Past Simple to talk about things that happened at a specific time in the past and that are now finished.

I met Grey Beaver three years ago.

Complete the letter by Weedon Scott's mother. Use the Present Perfect or Past Simple form of the verbs in brackets.

*White Fang a) ...has lived... (live) with us for two years now and, since 1914, he b) .... (become) one of our family. At the beginning, Collie c) .... (not like) him but now they d) .... (become) more friendly and they e) .... (have) six puppies together! White Fang f) .... (do) so many things for us: he g) .... (save) the life of my husband **and** my son! One day, Weedon h) .... (break) his leg in the woods and White Fang i) .... (come) to tell us about it. Also, late one evening, he j) .... (find) an escaped prisoner in our house. Sadly, my husband k) .... (shoot) White Fang, and he nearly l) .... (die). We m) .... (not forget) that night and we still talk about it.*

Since then, we n) .... (look after) him and he o) .... (begin) to walk again. He p) .... (not be) in the woods but he q) .... (see) his puppies.

GRAMMAR CHECK

Modal auxiliary verbs: mustn't and don't have to

In the affirmative, we use must or have to (both + infinitive without *to*) when we think it is necessary or very important to do something, or when it is an obligation.

We must find White Fang. We have to find White Fang.

In the negative, they have a different meaning. We use mustn't for prohibition.

You mustn't eat that food. (= Don't eat the food.)

We use don't have to for an absence of obligation.

You don't have to eat it. (= You can eat it if you want to, but it is not necessary.)

2 Choose the correct word or words to complete each sentence.

a Henry **mustn't**/**doesn't have to** leave the fire because the wolves are near him.

b The dogs **mustn't**/**don't have to** look for their food. The men give them meat.

c White Fang soon learns that he **mustn't**/**doesn't have to** bite the 'gods'.

d When he leaves Beauty Smith, White Fang **mustn't**/**doesn't have to** live in a cage.

e You **mustn't**/**don't have to** swim in the cold mountain river. It's dangerous.

f Now that Grey Beaver is rich, he **mustn't**/**doesn't have to** work every day.

3 Complete the sentences with *mustn't* or *doesn't/don't have to*.

a Never laugh at White Fang.

You *mustn't laugh at White Fang.*

b It is not necessary to feed him in the middle of the day.

You ....

c Don't give him bread.

You ....

d It is not necessary for him to stay in the house at night.

He ....

e Don't let him go upstairs.

He ....

GRAMMAR

GRAMMAR CHECK

Reflexive pronouns

We use reflexive pronouns – myself, yourself, himself, itself, herself, ourselves, yourselves, and themselves – when the subject and the object of a verb are the same.

Henry talked to himself during the long night.

The weasel hurt itself.

They kept themselves busy with work.

4 **Read Henry's diary. Complete the text with the words in the box.**

herself	himself	itself	yourselves
~~ourselves~~	themselves	myself	yourself

Tuesday

It's hard and lonely out here in the snowy woods and sometimes Bill and I sing to a) ...ourselves... for hours. At night, I close my eyes and think about my family. My mother is ill; she fell down the stairs and hurt b) .... just before I left. She was worried about my long journey. 'Look after c) ....,' she called when I left.

We started with six big strong dogs, but we now have only three. I thought that they could look after d) .... but, one by one, they have died – all killed by the wolves. One of the three dogs can't run well now because it cut e) .... on a stone last night.

Wednesday

This was a terrible day. One Ear ran away and some big wolves went after him. Bill chased them with his gun and a knife. Then I heard him scream. 'Perhaps he's hurt f) ....?' I asked g) .... But no. He was dead – killed by the wolves. Now I'm very worried. Will the wolves get me too?

Mother – if I die and you get this diary, remember that I love you and all my family. Look after h) .... when I have gone.

GRAMMAR

GRAMMAR CHECK

Reported questions with what, when, where, who, why, how much, and how many

In reported questions with what, when, where, who, why, how much, and how many, we put the subject before the verb, and we do not use *do* or *does*. The verb changes to the past with a past tense reporting verb. Pronouns change to match the speaker.

Direct question	Reported question
'What's that noise?' he asked.	He asked what that noise was.
'Where are you sleeping?' they asked.	They wanted to know where I was sleeping.
'Why is White Fang whining?' she asked.	She asked why White Fang was whining.
'How many wolves can you see?'	They wanted to know how many wolves I could see.

5   When Scott buys White Fang, Beauty Smith asks him a lot of questions. Scott later tells a friend all about it. Write the reported questions.

a Who are you?

Beauty Smith wanted to know .who I was.

e How much money do you have?

He wanted to know ....
....

b Where do you come from?

He wanted to know ....
....

f How much will you pay for the dog?

He asked me ....
....

c What do you want?

He asked me ....
....

g When can you pay the money?

He wanted to know ....
....

d Why are you interested in the wolf-dog?

He asked me ....
....

h Why are you looking so angry?

He asked me ....
....

GRAMMAR CHECK

Articles: a/an, the, and no article

We use the indefinite article a/an when we talk about singular nouns, and it is not clear which of many things we mean, or to begin describing someone or something.

Grey Beaver killed a wolf.　　　　　　*He was a big strong man.*

We use a in front of a word that begins with a consonant sound and an in front of a word that begins with a vowel sound.

It was a weasel.　　　　　　*It was an angry dog.*

We use the definite article the when we talk about singular and plural nouns, and it is clear which of many things we mean, or when we have already talked about it/them.

The she-wolf fell to the ground.

We use the plural + no article when we talk about nouns in general.

White Fang hunted animals.

6 Complete the text with *a/an*, *the*, or no article (–).

Beauty Smith was a) ..a.. small ugly man with yellow eyes. He
lived in b) .... old house with some other white men in
one of c) .... camps in Fort Yukon. But none of
d) .... other men liked him. They thought that he was
e) .... coward and f) .... very cruel man.
Beauty was interested in g) .... dogs. He loved
h) .... fighting dogs and he wanted to buy i) ....
wolf-dog. One day, he saw White Fang in j) .... fight. He
followed k) .... animal back home and tried to be friendly
to it.

White Fang didn't like Beauty Smith. And Grey Beaver didn't
want to sell l) .... dog to this man. Every time Smith
came along, White Fang sat on m) .... floor and growled.
But, one day, Beauty persuaded n) .... Indian to sell White Fang. He put
o) .... dog on p) .... long, thin piece of leather and tied him to
q) .... apple tree. White Fang knew that he had to escape. He couldn't stay with
this man.

GRAMMAR

GRAMMAR CHECK

Both and neither

We use both and neither when we talk about two things. Both has a positive meaning and neither has a negative meaning. We use neither before a singular noun.

Both dogs are thin. (= the two of them)   *Neither dog is fat.* (= not one of the two)

We use both of with the/these/them/Henry's etc.

Both of Henry's sleds are very slow.   *Both of them are very slow.*

We use neither of with the/these/them/Henry's etc. After *neither of*, a singular or a plural verb is possible. A singular verb is more formal.

Neither of Henry's sleds is/are fast.

We use both ... and but neither ... nor.

Both Bill and Henry are tired.   *Neither Scott nor his father has/have black hair.*

7 **Complete the sentences with *both* or *neither*.**

   a By the end of the long cold journey, ...both... the man and
   the wolf-dog were very tired.

   b The wolf had two cubs, but they were very ill and ....
   of them lived.

   c Scott said goodbye to .... of his parents at the door.

   d .... of the men were kind to the wolf and they gave it a lot of meat every day.

   e .... of Scott's children were very old. One was two and the other was four.

8 **Look at the table and write sentences using *Both ... and* or *Neither ... nor*.**

	Hair	Eyes	Other
Scott/Matt	brown ✓ black ✗	green ✓ blue ✗	kind ✓ cruel ✗

   a ...Both Scott and Matt have brown hair....

   b ....

   c ....

   d ....

   e ....

   f ....

66

GRAMMAR CHECK

Everywhere, nowhere, somewhere, and anywhere

We use everywhere to talk about 'in, at, on, or to all places'.

Grey Beaver chased Lip-lip everywhere.

There was snow everywhere.

We use nowhere to talk about 'in, at, on, or to no place'.

There was nowhere to stay in Fort Yukon.

'Where are you going?' 'Nowhere special.'

We use somewhere to talk about 'in, at, on, or to a place that we don't know exactly'.

He lives somewhere near the lake.

I put the money somewhere, but I can't find it.

We use anywhere to talk about 'in, at, on, or to any place'. We use it in negative sentences and in questions.

Henry couldn't find the dog anywhere.   *Did you go anywhere interesting?*

Choose the correct word to complete the sentences.

a After the fight, White Fang was tired and sat down. He didn't go **anywhere**/**nowhere**.

b White Fang loved Scott and he followed him **nowhere/everywhere**.

c 'Bill is dead,' said Henry. 'He died **somewhere/anywhere** near the trees.'

d White Fang couldn't find Grey Beaver **anywhere/everywhere**.

e Scott stood up on the steamer because there was **somewhere/nowhere** to sit.

f Dawson City is **anywhere/somewhere** on the other side of the river.

Complete the sentences with *everywhere, nowhere, somewhere*, or *anywhere*.

a White Fang looked *everywhere* for Collie, but he couldn't find her.

b The dog needed .... to hide because Beauty Smith was looking for him.

c They couldn't find .... to sleep that night.

d 'This place is beautiful,' said Scott. 'There's .... like it in the world.'

e There were a lot of wolves that night. Bill saw them .... that he looked.

67

DOMINOES
THE STRUCTURED APPROACH TO READING IN ENGLISH

Dominoes is an enjoyable series of illustrated classic and modern stories in four carefully graded language stages – from Starter to Three – which take learners from beginner to intermediate level.

Each *Domino* reader includes:
- a **good story** to read and enjoy
- **integrated activities** to develop reading skills and increase active vocabulary
- **personalized projects** to make the language and story themes more meaningful
- **seven pages of grammar activities** for consolidation.

Each *Domino* pack contains a reader, plus a MultiROM with:
- a **complete audio recording of the story**, fully dramatized to bring it to life
- **interactive activities** to offer further practice in reading and language skills and to consolidate learning.

If you liked this Level Two *Domino*, why not read these?

A Close Shave™
Aardman

When Wallace the inventor meets Wendolene in her wool shop, he falls in love with her at once. But why does her dog, Preston, hate Wallace's dog, Gromit?

Then, after Wallace's new sheep-shaving and pullover-making machine falls into the wrong hands, things start to go very wrong.

Can Gromit save Wallace from the danger of a 'close shave'?

Book ISBN: 978 0 19 424881 5
MultiROM Pack ISBN: 978 0 19 424833 4

Eight Great American Tales
O. Henry

What does a poor young woman do when she loses her boyfriend or wants to find one? What little lies do we tell to make ourselves look better in the eyes of those that we love? How can a friend save someone who is sure that they are going to die? What happens when someone's clever plans all go wrong? These sweetly surprising short stories – about both good times and bad – are sometimes sad, and sometimes funny. But all of them are sure to make you think.

Book ISBN: 978 0 19 424890 7
MultiROM Pack ISBN: 978 0 19 424842 6

You can find details and a full list of books in the *Dominoes* catalogue and Oxford English Language Teaching Catalogue, and on the website: www.oup.com/elt

Teachers: see www.oup.com/elt for a full range of online support, or consult your local office.

	CEF	Cambridge Exams	IELTS	TOEFL iBT	TOEIC
Starter	A1	YLE Movers	–	–	–
Level 1	A1–A2	YLE Flyers/KET	3.0	–	–
Level 2	A2–B1	KET-PET	3.0-4.0	–	–
Level 3	B1	PET	4.0	57-86	550